BUZZY AND THOMAS
MOVE INTO THE
PRESIDENT'S HOUSE

WRITTEN BY
VICKI TASHMAN

ILLUSTRATED BY
FÁTIMA STAMATO

To download your free Buzzy and Dickie coloring pages and to subscribe to my email list, please visit: http://www.historicaltails.com/free-coloring-download-page/

Published by Historical Tails
www.HistoricalTails.com

ISBN: 978-0-99720-940-2
        978-0-9972094-1-9 (ebook)

Library of Congress Control Number: 2016917722

Credits and permissions are listed on pages 38 and 39 and are considered a continuation of the copyright page.

CHAPTER ONE

Buzzy was a farm dog.

She loved everything about living on the big farm called Monticello, which was her home.

She loved the gardens full of flowers.

She loved her friends Caractacus the horse, Bull, the farm dog, and Dickie the bird.

But most of all, she loved living at Monticello with her owner, Thomas Jefferson.

They had lots in common.

Buzzy had gray fur and Thomas had gray hair.

Pony tail

gray hair

gray fur

tail

Long coat

Long coat of fur

2

Thomas wrote many letters, and Buzzy loved lying at his feet while he wrote them.

And they both loved walking around the land at Monticello.

One day, as they were walking, Thomas told her surprising news.

"I'm going to be president," he said, scratching her ear.

4

"We will need to move to the president's house in a town called Washington D.C.

It's a new house, just for presidents. John Adams lives there now.

But I'll be the new president, so I will live there and you will live there too."

5

CHAPTER TWO

Buzzy's tail stopped wagging.

She felt sad.

She felt afraid.

She felt confused.

Live somewhere else?

Away from the big fields full of good smells?

What about her friends Bull and Dickie?

And Caractacus with the soft nose?

She followed Thomas into the vegetable garden.

Surely Thomas would miss living on the farm too.

Thomas grew lots of his own food, including peas, lettuce, and asparagus.

Buzzy loved chewing on the asparagus spears.

Sometimes she had to step on the lettuce to reach them.

"Buzzy, you are stepping on my lettuce leaves," said Thomas. "Shoo!"

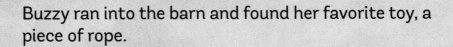

Buzzy ran into the barn and found her favorite toy, a piece of rope.

She carried it to Thomas.

She loved when Thomas pulled at her rope and she pulled back!

He grabbed the rope and threw it as far as he could.

Buzzy ran for it, ears flopping and tail flying.

But when she came back with it, Thomas had gone into the house.

CHAPTER THREE

Buzzy circled under a cherry tree and lay down.

Soon Caractacus the horse came along.

"Your ears are drooping, Buzzy," he said. "What's wrong?

"Thomas is going to be president and we're moving into the president's house," she said.

"But I don't want to leave Monticello."

And then her ears perked up. "Are you coming too, Caractacus?" she asked.

"I'll be taking Thomas to the president's house," said the horse, "and I'll be taking him back to Monticello when he visits.

But I won't be living there. I'm a farm horse.

Besides, I don't like the noise of the city."

Buzzy's ears felt even droopier.

"I can see you whenever I want to now, but when I move, I won't be able to," she said.

"I'm going to miss you, Caractacus."

CHAPTER FOUR

She was walking back to the house when she saw Bull, the farm's other dog.

"I'm moving into the president's house," she said. "Will you be moving too?"

"No," Bull said. "I take care of the other animals, so I need to stay here."

Buzzy loved Monticello, and the friends who lived there.

She wanted to stay.

BUT...She loved Thomas and wanted to be with him all the time.

And Thomas said he was leaving.

Dickie, Thomas's mockingbird was the only other animal allowed inside.

"Thomas and I are moving to the president's house," Buzzy said.

Her fluffy tail was between her legs.

"But I don't want to leave. I love Monticello. I love Caractacus and Bull.

I love you too, Dickie. How will I leave all my friends?

Where will I sleep in the president's house?

Where will I eat?

Where will I play and run?"

Dickie hopped from one foot to the other.

"I don't know the answers to your questions," said Dickie.

CHAPTER FIVE

Thomas came into the room.

"Come along, Buzzy," he said. "We're going to look at our new home."

He got into the carriage.

Caractacus was pulling the carriage. He neighed when he saw Buzzy and Dickie.

Buzzy jumped into the back seat with Thomas.

She didn't want to see the new house.

But she wanted to be with Thomas.

And she loved carriage rides.

Dickie flew to Thomas's shoulder.

"What are you doing here?" laughed Thomas.

Dickie let out a big "chirp, chirp, chirp!"

They passed green fields and farm animals.

Buzzy barked at goats.

She barked at cows.

And she barked at chickens.

It was a fun carriage ride.

CHAPTER SIX

Finally, they arrived at the president's house.

President John Adams greeted them at the front door. He shook Thomas's hand.

"I see you brought some friends," said John. "Let me show you around the house."

In the front room Buzzy saw tall windows and a big desk.

There was a river outside and lots of books on the shelves.

She loved the smell of books.

Under the desk was a perfect place for her to lie down while Thomas was working.

They went upstairs to the president's bedroom.

A big comfy bed was in the middle of the room.

"I could put my sleeping pillow here," Buzzy thought.

They went outside.

She didn't see a vegetable garden, but there was a green lawn and large trees.

"This is a nice place to run around!" she said to Dickie.

CHAPTER SEVEN

Moving day finally came.

Buzzy barked at the moving men.

But they just patted her on the head.

"I will move my sleeping pillow myself!" she barked at them in Thomas's bedroom.

She grabbed the pillow, pulled it downstairs and put it in a crate herself.

Then she went into the kitchen and found her bowl.

She put that in the crate too.

I have one more thing to put in the crate, she thought.

She ran outside and sniffed. She ran to the front yard. She ran to the back yard.

Where was it? Where was her favorite rope toy?

Finally, she found it under the cherry tree.

"Here it is!" she said and she picked up the toy and dropped it into the crate.

Thomas picked up Buzzy's crate and put it in the carriage.

"Let's go!" he said.

CHAPTER EIGHT

When they arrived at the president's house, Buzzy saw lots of men and women working.

They were helping get them settled in the new house.

A man brought Buzzy's crate into the front room.

She saw her bowl inside the crate so she took it into the kitchen.

She pulled out her sleeping pillow and dragged it upstairs into Thomas's bedroom.

She put the pillow on the side of the big bed.

"This is where I'll sleep every night," she said to herself.

Back downstairs, she grabbed her toy rope from the crate and looked for Thomas.

Thomas was sitting at his desk.

She lay down at his feet. Her new spot felt safe and warm.

She heard a sound and her ears perked up.

"Chirp, chirp, chirp!"

There was Dickie's birdcage, hanging by the window with Dickie chirping inside!

"Dickie, you're living in the president's house too!" Buzzy said.

She waved her fluffy tail and barked.

"I loved living at Monticello, but I know I'm going to love living at the president's house!"

VARIOUS FACTS

All the names in this book are real.
Thomas Jefferson became President of the United States in 1801 and moved into the President's House (That's what they called the White House back then).
Thomas Jefferson had a dog named Buzzy. He brought her home from France. Buzzy was a new breed of dog in the United States, a Briard.
Thomas Jefferson wrote of the Briard, "They are the finest house and farm dogs I have ever seen." *
Jefferson had a horse named Caractacus and another dog named Bull.
He also had a pet mockingbird named Dickie.
Many people wrote about Dickie. **

*Thomas Jefferson and dogs: https://www.monticello.org/site/house-and-gardens/dogs
**Thomas Jefferson's bird, Dickie: http://www.eyewitnesstohistory.com/jeffersonwhitehouse.htm

For more information about Thomas Jefferson, Buzzy and Monticello, please visit the Historical Tails website at http://www.historicaltails.com

A Bird That Whistles: In Jefferson's Cabinet, 1803,
by Peter Waddell for the White House Historical Association

This is a painting of Thomas Jefferson and his friend,
James Madison in the Oval Office.
Can you see Dickie in this painting?
Where is Dickie's birdcage?
Where is Buzzy hiding?

A *special thanks* to my family and friends who helped me create, craft, refine and learn about writing, and researching pets of historical figures. Extra special thanks to my wonderful husband, Rich who supports me in all my endeavors. And a big hug goes to my sweet golden retrievers, Ricky and Georgia. They are my inspiration.

To download your free Buzzy and Dickie coloring pages and to subscribe to my email list, please visit:

http://www.historicaltails.com/ free-coloring-download-page/

CPSIA information can be obtained
at www.ICGtesting.com
Printed in the USA
LVOW01s0925270417
532387LV00003B/5/P

9 780997 209402